Written by Gill Davies and Lynne Gibbs
Illustrated by Rachael O'Neill and Melanie Mitchell

Published by Brimax,
A division of Autumn Publishing Limited
©2004 Autumn Publishing Limited
Appledram Barns, Chichester PO20 7EQ

Printed in China

My Little
Animal
Storybook
Treasury

Written by

Gill Davies
& Lynne Gibbs

Illustrated by

Rachael O'Neill
& Melanie Mitchell

First published as:

Can't, Shan't, Won't! © Octopus Publishing Group 2001

Tiny's Big Wish © Octopus Publishing Group 2001

Rory's Story © Octopus Publishing Group 2001

Ping Won't Share © Octopus Publishing Group 2002

Schooltime for Sammy © Octopus Publishing Group 2002

Quiet as a Mouse © Octopus Publishing Group 2002

This edition first published in Great Britain in 2002 by Brimax,
an imprint of Octopus Publishing Group Ltd
2-4 Heron Quays, London E14 4JP
© Octopus Publishing Group Ltd

A CIP catalogue record for this book is available
from the British Library.

ISBN 1 85854 590 0

Printed in Italy

❊ Contents ❊

Note to Parents

The Growing Pains series is specially designed to help young children make sense of the world around them. Each story has a gentle moral lesson that aims to help young readers deal with new situations in a positive and happy manner. Popular themes such as starting school, sibling rivalry, and shyness are sensitively explored in these beautifully illustrated stories. After sharing each story with your child, take time to ask and answer questions, and to relate the story to your child's own life.

Rory's Story

Rory the tiger is having a terrible time!
He has a new baby sister.
She is very small and cries a lot, and
she waves little, clenched paws in the air.
Rory does not know what to think of her.
She is too small to play with him.
He is afraid to hold her in case she slips.
Now his mother and father are always busy.

"Will you cuddle me?" asks Rory.
"In a minute," says Mother Tiger.
"First I have to feed the baby."
Rory waits...
"Will you cuddle me now?" asks Rory.
"Soon," says Mother Tiger.
"First I have to wash the baby's ears."
Rory waits...

"Will you give me a ride on your back?"
asks Rory.
"Soon," says Mother Tiger.
"First I have to wash the baby's face."
Rory waits...
"Will you give me a ride on your
back now?" asks Rory.
"Soon," says Mother Tiger.
"First I have to wash the baby's tail."
Rory sighs and goes to see if his father
will play with him.

"Will you climb a tree with me?"
Rory asks Father Tiger.
"Soon," says Father Tiger,
"but first I have to finish tidying the den."
Rory waits...

"Will you climb a tree now?"
asks Rory.
"Soon," says Father Tiger. "First I have
to teach the baby how to growl.
Do you want to help?"
"No," says Rory, feeling a little bit
left out, and sad, and bored.
Everyone is so busy.

Rory goes outside. Hippo comes
bouncing along the path.
"Hi!" says Hippo.
"Shall we play a game?"
"Okay," says Rory, grinning,
"what shall we play?"

Crocodiles!

They have a fun game!

First Hippo pretends
to be a crocodile
chasing Rory.

Then Rory pretends
to be a crocodile
chasing Hippo.

The two friends run in circles until they fall over,
laughing and kicking their legs in the air.
They pretend to SNAP! big crocodile teeth.
SNIP SNAP! Growwwl!

Mother Tiger opens the door,
looking angry.
"Ssshh, you two!" she says.
"You are making too much noise.
You will wake the baby...
there, she is crying already."

Mother Tiger goes back indoors.
Rory and Hippo can hear
the little cub crying, but after
a while the sound stops.

"Let's take a look," says Hippo,
"I haven't seen your new baby sister yet."
So they tip-toe inside.
Mother Tiger is holding the baby
and singing softly to her.

"Hush little tiger, don't growl and cry,
Mama's going to sing you a lullaby.
The jungle is green, the sky is blue,
Your brother Rory wants to cuddle you."

"No I don't!" says Rory.
"I don't know how."
"It's easy," says Mother Tiger.
"Sit down and I'll show you."
Mother Tiger brings the baby over to Rory.
Suddenly, there is Rory's new baby sister,
all cuddled up on his lap.
She feels warm and soft. She smiles.
Rory smiles back.

"You're nice," says Rory.
His baby sister makes a gurgly growl back.
She clasps his paw tight. Then she closes her
eyes and falls asleep. Mother Tiger puts the
baby back into her snug corner of the den.

Rory and Hippo creep back outside
to play a quiet game.
"She's okay, my baby sister,"
says Rory to Hippo.
"She's cute," says Hippo.
"You're lucky, Rory."

Now Rory tells everyone in the jungle
about his new baby sister.
"She's soft and warm!" he says.
"She can clench her fists!" he smiles.
"And she's got a gurgly growl" he grins.
Then he practices his own lullaby
to sing to his little sister.

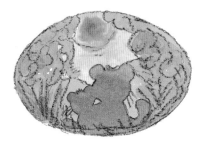

"Hush little sister, don't cry at all,
Rory will hold you so you won't fall.
The jungle is green, the sky is blue,
Your brother Rory is proud of you."

Ping Won't Share

Ping and his friends, Shi Shi and Yang, were
very hungry. The pandas' favourite food was bamboo,
but their supply was running out. They searched the
forest high and low, with their tummies rumbling,
but they couldn't find any more bamboo.
"What will we do if we never find any food?"
cried Shi Shi.

"Let's look one more time," said Yang. "We'll go in separate directions and meet back here later."

Ping trudged through the forest searching for food, but hunger made him tired so he headed home for a nap. He could not believe his luck when he found a large patch of bamboo growing near his home.

Sitting under a tree, Ping munched his way through a leafy pile of bamboo, then rubbed his full tummy and sighed happily.
This will last me for days, thought Ping.
But I won't tell anyone else what I've found, otherwise they might want to share it too.

Later, just as the sun was going down,
Ping and his friends sat in a circle and shared
their last branch of bamboo. Ping took just a
small bite and left the rest for the others.
"How do you stay so big and strong when you
eat so little, Ping?" asked Yang.
"Oh, I don't need much food," replied Ping,
thinking guiltily of his secret dinner.

When his friends were sound asleep
that night, Ping lay wide awake.
*I am being greedy keeping all that bamboo
far myself*, thought Ping. He resolved to
share the bamboo with his friends.

But the next morning, when Ping's tummy
rumbled, he quickly changed his mind.
Sneaking away, Ping crept to the pile
of bamboo he had collected and had a
breakfast feast, all by himself.

Ping's friends sadly decided it was time
to leave their homes and travel
far away in search of food.
"I know where you can find bamboo,"
squawked a nosy pheasant, perched on
a branch. The bird pointed his wing towards
a snow-covered peak in the distance.
"It grows on that mountainside," he said.

When Ping told his friends that he was not
leaving with them, they looked very sad.
"I am happy here and I don't need much
food to keep me fit and strong," lied Ping.

Waving goodbye, Yang and Shi Shi
set off on their long journey.
"I hope you find lots of *bamboo*," called Ping.
As he watched them leave, Ping wished he could have
given his friends just a little *bamboo* for their trip.
"But if I had, they would have asked where
it came from," said Ping with a sigh.
"And I wouldn't want to share it ALL."

At first, Ping was quite happy. He had the birds and the butterflies to keep him company, and there was plenty to eat. But as the days passed, Ping's supply of bamboo grew smaller and smaller, until one day there was nothing left. Ping rubbed his rumbling tummy and thought about his friends in their new home.

One afternoon, as Ping searched for tiny scraps
of bamboo, the pheasant swooped down.
"It's a pity you didn't go with your friends,"
chirped the bird. "They found lots
of bamboo and cosy new homes."
"If only I had shared my bamboo,"
whimpered a lonely and hungry Ping.
"I wouldn't be all alone with nothing to eat."

Settling back down in his favourite spot,
Ping remembered how much fun he used
to have playing with Shi Shi and Yang.
He missed their games of hide-and-seek.

Big tears began to roll down his face as
he remembered how badly he had treated
his friends. He was soon sobbing so loudly
that he did not hear two familiar voices
calling out, "Hello, Ping!"

"Don't cry, Ping," said Shi Shi and Yang as they gathered around him. "We've come back to share the bamboo that we found." Wiping away his tears, Ping jumped to his feet and hugged his friends.

"I've missed you two so much!" he cried. Ping felt very ashamed of his selfishness and told his friends all about the supply of bamboo he had kept for himself.

Yang and Shi Shi could hardly believe
what they were hearing.
"How could you just let us go hungry?"
demanded Yang angrily.
"You've been very selfish,"
said Shi Shi, shaking her head.

"I am so sorry," wailed Ping. "Will you please
forgive me?" He looked very sad and sorry.

Realising that Ping had truly learned his lesson,
his friends forgave him. They shared some of the
bamboo they had brought with Ping, for
he would need strength for the journey ahead.
"From now on, we'll always stick together," said Shi Shi.
"From now on, I'll always share with
my friends," promised Ping.
Munching their bamboo happily, the three
pandas watched the sun set together.

Can't, Shan't, Won't!

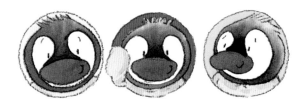

In a land of ice and snow,
where the wild wind blows, live three very
naughty penguins. They are called
Can't, Shan't and Won't.
Whenever Mother Penguin asks the little
rascals to help her, they shuffle
and slither away as fast as they
can on their slippery,
flippery feet, and
pretend not to hear her.

Today Mother Penguin wants the little
penguins to catch some fish for supper.
As soon as they hear her calling,
"Can't... Shan't... Won't!"
the naughty penguins race down the slippery
slide and hide in an ice cave.
But Mother Penguin is pretty good at sliding
too, and very good at finding ice caves,
so she soon catches them out.

"Now!" gasps Mother Penguin,
shaking the snow from her flipper-like
wings and panting for breath.
"I need your help. You must catch
some big, fat, juicy fish for supper."
The three little penguins
look up at her sadly.

"Can't," says Can't.
"My flippers are too cold."
"Shan't!" says Shan't. "My feet are too cold."
"Won't!" says Won't. "My beak is too cold."
"Nonsense!" says Mother Penguin.
"You are penguins. You like the cold!
Now here are your fishing rods -
off you go."

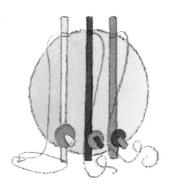

So the three little penguins slide
off across the snow. Icy Lake is always
frozen over, but every now and then there
are little round holes which the seals use
to come up for air. These holes are perfect
for patient penguins to catch fish from.
But Can't, Shan't and Won't are not
patient. They cannot sit still
for a minute.

"I can't *see* the point in sitting here,"
says Can't, after just one minute,
peering into the hole.
"I shan't *be able* to catch a thing," says
Shan't after just two minutes.
"My line is tangled up."
"I won't ever *be* warm again," says Won't,
after just three minutes, and
shivering from his *beak* to his feet.
"Let's go home!"
shout Can't, Shan't and Won't.
So they set off across the ice,
without a single fish.

"Can't go home without fish, Mother will
be cross," says Can't, slipping on the ice.
"Shan't have anything for supper!"
says Shan't, sliding down an icy bank.
"Won't go home again,"
says Won't, skating on one foot.
So they decide to run away!

The little penguins skip and scamper all the
way to where the icy land meets the sea.
There they jump onto an iceberg, and before
very long, the iceberg slides away,
floating along on the waves.

The little penguins are very scared.
What's your name" asks an old walrus.
"Can't!" cries Can't. "Can't ever stop!"
"What's your name?" asks a snowy seal.
"Shan't!" sobs Shan't.
"Shan't ever get home!"
"What's your name?" booms a huge whale.
"Won't!" weeps Won't.
"Won't ever run away again!"

Still the iceberg sails on. Soon it
is dark, and the moon rises over the
snow-capped sea. It is very cold, and
by now the penguins are very very scared!
Then suddenly the wild wind begins to blow.
It blows the iceberg in a circle.
It blows the iceberg across the waves.
It blows the iceberg back to shore,
where the icy land meets the sea.
And there, waiting for the
little penguins, is Mother.

"Thank goodness you're safe!"
She hugs each little penguin in turn.
"We were lost!" cries Can't.
"We were cold!" sobs Shan't.
"And we haven't any fish!" weeps Won't.
"Never mind," says Mother Penguin.
"Father has caught plenty, so we can have
a nice fish supper. Let's go home."
Off they ride on Father's sledge, back to
their warm, safe house in the snow.

After supper Mother tucks the penguins
into their warm cosy bed.
"I can't believe we were so silly," sighs Can't.
"I can," laughs Mother Penguin.
"We shan't run away again,"
mumbles Shan't.
"Home is the best place to be,"
agrees Mother.
"And we won't ever be naughty again!"
yawns Won't, with just a hint of a twinkle
in his one open eye.
"We'll see!" smiles Mother Penguin.
"Sweet dreams, Can't, Shan't, Won't".

Schooltime for Sammy

While his brother and sister got ready for the first day of school, Sammy was busy playing. He climbed his favourite tree and swung from branch to branch. Pushing books into his satchel, Fred called up, "You're old enough to go to school this year, Sammy." "I don't want to go to school! I want to stay home and play!" replied Sammy.

"But school is fun, and you'll learn all
kinds of things," said Sophie.
"I'm not going!" said Sammy, dangling upside
down and pulling a face. "I already know
everything. I know how to climb all the tallest
trees and I can swing really fast.
So there! Catch me if you can!"
But Fred and Sophie didn't chase after him –
they didn't want to be late for school.

Sammy spent the morning playing but soon
got bored without any playmates.
"What's wrong, Sammy?" asked his mother,
when she found him moping.
"There's nobody to play with," said Sammy grumpily.
"Well, your friends are all at school," explained
his mum. "Maybe you should go, too."
"No way!" shouted Sammy,
scrambling back up the tree.

At last, Sophie and Fred returned home,
chattering excitedly about their busy day. Sammy
ran to greet them with an after-school snack.

Sammy wanted Fred and Sophie to play with him,
but they said that they had homework to do.
Sammy did not want to be left out.
"I can do homework," he said, climbing onto
a chair and joining them at the table,
"How many days are there in April?" Fred asked Sophie.
"Twenty five ninety zillion!" shouted Sammy, trying to help
"Oh, Sammy, don't be silly. We're trying to work,"
said Sophie with a sigh.

When Sammy's friend Jack came to visit,
he was full of news about his new school.
"The teacher is really nice and I've learned lots
of important things," said Jack proudly.
"I know what two plus one plus two is."
"So do I!" said Sammy,
trying to count on his fingers.
"What is it, then?" asked Jack.
"It's, um, it's... a lot!" he answered.
"You don't know!" exclaimed Jack.

"I even learned how to write my own name,"
Jack continued. He picked up a stick.
With his tongue clenched between his teeth,
he carefully wrote J-A-C-K in the dirt.

"I can write my name too. Look!" said Sammy.
"That's not writing, that's just *scribble*!" scoffed Jack.
Poor Sammy felt rather embarrassed.

Now Sammy was quite curious about school.
"What else did you do at school, Jack?" he asked.
"Well, I made lots of new friends and we
all played games together," said Jack.

As Sammy listened, Jack told him everything
that he had learned. His favourite part of the day
was Show and Tell, when people could bring in
special things and share them with the class.
"You really did do a lot,"
said Sammy with a sad sigh.

"I'll paint you a picture of a tree, if you
want," offered Jack, to cheer up his friend.
"That's another thing I learned today!"
Hardly blinking in case he missed anything,
Sammy watched as Jack brushed
paint over a piece of paper.
"That's the best picture in the whole world!"
said Sammy admiringly.

When Jack had gone, Sammy tried to draw
a tree himself, but his painting just
looked like a messy blob.

That night at dinner, Sammy was very quiet.
He did not even feel like eating his dinner.
Nobody noticed, though, because Sophie and Fred
were chattering loudly about school.
"I got a gold star on my spelling test," bragged Sophie.
"I won a race at playtime," said Fred proudly.
"Well done, both of you," said their mother and father.

After dinner, Sammy decided that he wanted to be as clever as his brother and sister.
Very quietly, he crept over to Sophie's school satchel and slipped out a book.
Sitting in a corner, he opened the book and tried to read it. But it was no use – the words just looked like squiggles to him.

When Sophie and Fred found Sammy with the book, they read him the story. It was a thrilling tale about pirates.

The next morning, Sammy woke up very early.
He was very excited as he searched for the
little satchel that his mother had made for him.
When he found it, he packed Effalump,
his favourite toy, carefully inside.
He wanted to have something for Show and Tell.
Sammy marched into the kitchen
and announced, "I'm ready!"

Sammy's family looked up in surprise.
"Ready for what, Sammy?" asked his father.
"I want to go to school after all," declared
Sammy. "I want to learn how to read and write
and count and draw beautiful pictures."
"That's wonderful," said his mother.
"But first you'll need to have some breakfast."

After breakfast, Sammy set off with Sophie
and Fred, walking at a very quick pace.
"I'm already a day late for school," said Sammy
with a grin. "I don't want to miss any more!"

Tiny's
Big Wish

In Africa, where the grass
grows high and the ostriches stretch
their necks to see across the plains,
the elephants are marching.

"Hup, two, three, four!
We elephants are very sure:
Sure that we are big and strong,
With enormous ears and trunks so long.
We're always brave, we're always bold...
We're always warm and never cold!
Hup, two, three, four!
Who could ask for anything more?"

On and on the elephants march,
down to the river to drink. But not all of
the elephants are *big* and *strong*. Not all
of them are *brave* and *bold*. There is one
elephant who is very small.
He has little baby legs that cannot march
quickly enough, so he is always
running behind the others.

This is Tiny.

Tiny trips over his little elephant feet.
Then he trips over his little elephant trunk.
His mother waits for him to catch her up
and takes him down to the river.

"Oh dear," sighs Tiny as his
mother scrubs his back.
"I wish I was big. I wish I was strong.
I wish I was brave. And I wish
I could march in time."

Then Tiny sings his own sad, little song:

"Little is such a hard thing to be,
Everyone else is bigger than me.
I wish I was brave,
I wish I was strong,
I wish my trunk was ever so long!
I wish I could march:
Hup, two, three, four,
And not be a baby anymore."

His mother smiles as she sprays
Tiny's lovely little face with fresh, cool water.
"Don't worry, Tiny," she says.
"Once, we were all ever so little too!
One day you will be big and strong
just like all the other elephants."

Tiny looks up at his mother.
He looks up from her big, wrinkly
knees to her big, crinkly ears; from her
bright, blinking eyes to the top of her
great, domed head.

"As big as you?" he asks.
"Bigger!" says his mother.

But Tiny wanders off shaking
his head sadly, because he doesn't
quite believe her.

"I wish I was big and had an enormous
great body just like you!" says Tiny
to the old water buffalo.
"Don't worry, Tiny," says Buffalo.
"One day your body will be enormous too."
Tiny looks up at him.
He looks up from Buffalo's great long mane
to his curled long horns, right to the top
of his great hairy head.
"As big as yours?" he asks.
"Bigger!" says Buffalo
But Tiny wanders off shaking his head
sadly. He doesn't quite believe it!

"I wish I was big and had a gigantic great belly just like you!" says Tiny to Harry the hippo.

"Don't worry, Tiny," says Harry.

"One day your belly will be enormous too."

Tiny looks up at him. He looks up from Harry's huge feet to his great, yawning mouth, to the top of Harry's enormous flat head. "As big as yours?" he asks.

"Bigger!" says Harry.

But still Tiny does not quite believe him!

He decides to ask some of the other animals.
"Will I be as tall as you one day?"
Tiny asks Ostrich.
"Taller!" says Ostrich.
"Hmm!" says Tiny, thinking hard.

"Will I be bigger than you one day?"
Tiny asks Zebra.
"Of course!" says Zebra, laughing.
"Will I really be big and tall one day?"
Tiny asks the lions and scampering warthogs.
"Of course!" they all say, and smile
at the little elephant.

Tiny goes back to the herd, who are all busy
munching and chomping to keep themselves
big and strong. Finally Tiny believes
what he has been told.

"I will be bigger than you one day,"
Tiny tells his mother.
"I will be stronger than you one day,"
Tiny tells his big sister.
"I'll have a longer trunk than you one day,"
Tiny tells his aunt.
"We know," they all laugh together.

This time, as the herd marches off, Tiny stomps along proudly beside his mother, and he sings his new song.

"Being so little is not so bad,
It's not for ever, so I won't be sad.
I will be brave, I will be strong,
I will have a trunk that's ever so long!
I'll march in time:
Hup, two, three, four,
And not be the baby anymore."

And now, all the elephants agree, Tiny will be the biggest, bravest elephant of them all!

Quiet as a Mouse

It was a very exciting morning in the Mouse House
when three little envelopes plopped onto the doormat.
"A party!" cried Holly and Polly, tearing open
their invitations. "We'll all have a great time."
But Molly did not agree with her sisters. She was so
shy that she blushed if another mouse so much
as twitched his whiskers at her.
"I can't possibly go!" she squeaked.

"You poor thing," said Holly, when she saw Molly.
Her whole face was covered in big, red spots.
"Are you ill?" asked Polly.
"I really don't think that I should go to the
party now," said Molly weakly.
"Oh, you'll be fine," said Mother.
"As long as you wash those spots off first."
She smiled and picked up the red crayon that
Molly had used to draw on the spots.

While her sisters got ready for the party,
Molly desperately tried to think of another plan.
She decided to hide where nobody could find her.
Crawling under her bed, Molly curled up into a tiny ball.
"Molly, where are you?" called her sisters.
She held her breath and kept very, very still.

It was very dusty underneath Molly's
bed and a piece of fluff tickled her nose.
Soon, she could not hold back any longer.
"ATISHOO!" she sneezed loudly.
"ATISHOO! ATISHOO! ATISHOO!"

"We know where you are," said Holly and Polly
as they peeked under the bed.
"What are you doing?" they asked, giggling.
Feeling silly, Molly crawled out from under her
bed. There must be something else she could do!

"Hurry up, Molly," said Mother, when she saw
her sitting on her bed. "It's almost time for the party."
Molly just sat there, looking forlorn.
"What's the matter?" asked Mother.
Molly held up a piece of paper. It read, "I can't
possibly go to the party. I have lost my squeak."
"Oh dear," tutted Mother. "That is a shame.
I'll go and get some medicine for you."

"Poor you," said Holly, hiding a smile.
"Mother's medicine tastes really horrible."
"I'm glad I don't have to take it," said Polly.
"We're going to have so much fun at the party."

Molly thought for a little while.
Then she gave a little cough and whispered,
"Actually, I think my squeak has just come back.
Perhaps I will go to the party after all."
"Don't worry, we'll stay with you all the time,"
said her sisters.

When they arrived at the party, Molly, Holly, and Polly were soon surrounded by lots of other little mice. "Remember what you promised," Molly squeaked, feeling her cheeks getting redder and redder and hotter and hotter. "Please don't leave me on my own."

"We promise," said Holly and Polly.

"Oh, I wish I was at home," Molly whispered.

Music began to play and the fun began. Molly
was soon caught up in a group of dancing mice.
"Oh, no!" she gasped.
Molly looked around nervously for her sisters,
but soon her feet began to move to
the music. Around and around she whirled
and twirled with the other mice.
"Where is she?" asked Holly, worriedly.

Just then, Molly danced past her sisters.
"This party is fun!" she called.
"Why don't you two join in?"

Forgetting about being shy, Molly
soon made lots of new friends.

"I can't believe that this is our shy little sister,"
said Polly proudly, as Molly joined in
a game of blind man's bluff.
Wearing a blindfold, Molly searched for the
other mice, bumping into things as she went.
"Got you!" she cried, finding someone
hiding behind a tree.

"Let's play another game!" suggested Molly.
"What shall we play?" asked her new friends.
Molly thought for a while, then exclaimed,
"I know! How about musical chairs?"
The little mice ran round and round a row of chairs.

When the music stopped, Molly rushed to
find a seat but ended up sitting on the ground!
"Whoops!" she said with a giggle.

When it was time to leave, Molly was sad to go.
"I wish we could stay longer," she said with a sigh.
"There will be other parties," Polly assured her.
"I must say goodbye to everyone,"
said Molly, rushing back.

Polly and Holly had to lead Molly from the party.
"Bye, everyone!" called Molly.
"See you again soon."

Back home, Molly told Mother all about the
wonderful time they had had at the party.
"We danced and played games and made lots
of new friends," she reported enthusiastically.
"I knew that you would enjoy it," said Mother.
"Molly was the life of the party," said Holly and Polly.
"I had so much fun," said Molly,
"I'm not so shy after all."

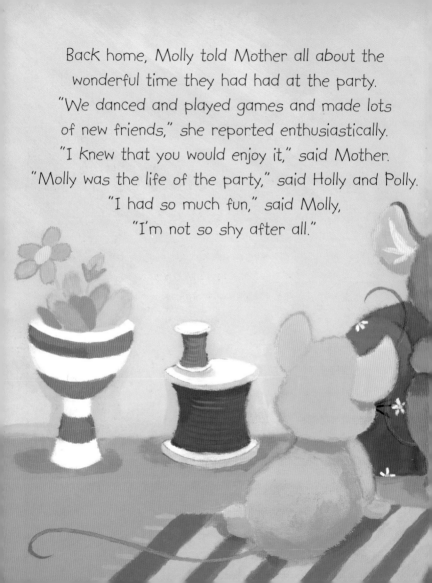